JER Stephe
Stephens, Elle,
One fancy day /
$5.99
on1350283120

3   4028   11016   0588
HARRIS COUNTY PUBLIC LIBRARY

D0834344

STEP INTO READING® will help your c s
five steps to reading success. Each step i
art or photographs. In addition to original
characters, there are Step into Reading No , nonics Readers
and Boxed Sets, Sticker Readers, and Comic Readers—a complete literacy
program with something to interest every child.

Learning to Read, Step by Step

Ready to Read   Preschool–Kindergarten
• big type and easy words • rhyme and rhythm • picture clues
For children who know the alphabet and are eager to
begin reading.

Reading with Help   Preschool–Grade 1
• basic vocabulary • short sentences • simple stories
For children who recognize familiar words and sound out
new words with help.

Reading on Your Own   Grades 1–3
• engaging characters • easy-to-follow plots • popular topics
For children who are ready to read on their own.

Reading Paragraphs   Grades 2–3
• challenging vocabulary • short paragraphs • exciting stories
For newly independent readers who read simple sentences
with confidence.

Ready for Chapters   Grades 2–4
• chapters • longer paragraphs • full-color art
For children who want to take the plunge into chapter books
but still like colorful pictures.

STEP INTO READING® is designed to give every child a successful
reading experience. The grade levels are only guides; children will progress
through the steps at their own speed, developing confidence in their reading.

Remember, a lifetime love of reading starts with a single step!

© 2023 Viacom International Inc. All Rights Reserved. Nickelodeon, SpongeBob SquarePants, and all related titles, logos, and characters are trademarks of Viacom International Inc. Published in the United States by Random House Children's Books, a division of Penguin Random House LLC, 1745 Broadway, New York, NY 10019, and in Canada by Penguin Random House Canada Limited, Toronto.

Step into Reading, Random House, and the Random House colophon are registered trademarks of Penguin Random House LLC.

created by

Stephen Hillenburg

Visit us on the Web!
StepIntoReading.com
rhcbooks.com

Educators and librarians, for a variety of teaching tools, visit us at RHTeachersLibrarians.com

ISBN 978-0-593-43179-5 (trade) — ISBN 978-0-593-43180-1 (lib. bdg.)

Printed in the United States of America

10 9 8 7 6 5 4 3 2 1

STEP 3 INTO READING®
STEP READING ON YOUR OWN

nickelodeon

KAMP KORAL
SPONGEBOB'S UNDER YEARS

One Fancy Day

by Elle Stephens

based on the teleplay "My Fair Nobby"
by Andrew Goodman

illustrated by Dave Aikins

Random House 🏠 New York

One day at Kamp Koral,
SpongeBob and Patrick
are doing arts and crafts.
Their friend Narlene visits.

SpongeBob shows her
the sweater he made.
He sees Narlene's bag.
"Are you running away?"
he asks her.

Narlene says she is

not running away.

She is going to the family feud.

It is a big fight

between families.

She opens her bag.
Her baby brother,
Nobby, pops out!
He is too young for the feud.
"Do you think you could keep
an eye on him until I'm back?"
she asks SpongeBob and Patrick.

SpongeBob and Patrick say yes.

They are excited!

"Good luck!" says Narlene.

"He can get a little wild."

SpongeBob makes Nobby

a camp kerchief.

But Nobby is gone!

He uses arts and crafts supplies
to make a giant spiderweb.

He begins to trap
other campers in it!
SpongeBob and Patrick stop him.

"Nobby does seem a tad frisky,"
says SpongeBob.
Patrick has an idea.
They will tire Nobby out
with lots of camp activities.
Then he will calm down.

They take him
to the slap line.

Nobby races ahead.
He pushes everyone
off the line
and into the water!

SpongeBob and Patrick take Nobby
to Jelly Meadows.
They teach him
to catch jellyfish.

Nobby rides the jellyfish instead.
He shoots bolts
from its tentacles!

Nobby zaps SpongeBob
and Patrick.

Then he rides the jellyfish
all over the camp.
He zaps the cabins
and sets them on fire!

SpongeBob and Patrick
look for Nobby.
They find him in a cabin
getting a manners lesson.
He learns to eat and speak
and sit nicely.

Nobby is not wild anymore!
SpongeBob and Patrick
are shocked.

The next day,
Narlene comes back.
She finds Nobby
wearing fancy clothes
and sitting very still.
She can't believe it!

Narlene does not like
fancy Nobby.
She misses her wild
baby brother.
Patrick has an idea.

The friends take Nobby
into the woods.
They show him his favorite
chewing tree.
He does not want
to chew.

They give him his favorite
sugary drink.
He would rather drink water.
He does not want
to be wild anymore.

Narlene has one last idea.

If Nobby will not be wild for her,

she will be fancy for him.

She takes a bath.

She gets new clothes.

Soon Narlene is ready.
She looks very fancy.
Patrick helps her find Nobby.
"Allow me to introduce
the new Narlene!" he says.

Just then, Nobby rips off
his fancy clothes.
"Best prank ever!" he shouts.
He was playing a trick
on Narlene the whole time!

Narlene can't believe it.
She is so proud of Nobby!
She tells him that he can go
to the next family feud.

"A prank that big proves you're ready," she says. Nobby is excited!

Harris County Public Library, Houston, TX

What a wild day!